D0923271

CLAWED!

An Up2U Horror Adventure

By: Dotti Enderle
Illustrated by: Vivienne To

magic wagon

visit us at www.abdopublishing.com

Printed in the United States of America, North Mankato, Minnesota.
052013
092013

 This book contains at least 10% recycled materials.

Written by Dotti Enderle
Illustrated by Vivienne To
Edited by Stephanie Hedlund and Rochelle Baltzer
Cover and interior design by Neil Klinepier

Library of Congress Cataloging-in-Publication Data

Enderle, Dotti, 1954-
  Clawed! : an Up2U horror adventure / By Dotti Enderle ; Illustrated by Vivienne To.
     p. cm. -- (Up2U adventures)
  Summary: After he is clawed by a stray, Tray finds himself turning into a cat every night, so he sets out to find the old gray tomcat called Honcho who can reverse the curse, and the reader is invited to choose between three possible outcomes.
  ISBN 978-1-61641-965-3
  1. Plot-your-own stories. 2. Shapeshifting--Juvenile fiction. 3. Feral cats--Juvenile fiction. 4. Horror tales. [1. Shapeshifting--Fiction. 2. Feral cats--Fiction. 3. Cats--Fiction. 4. Horror stories. 5. Plot-your-own stories.] I. To, Vivienne, ill. II. Title.
  PZ7.E69645Cl 2013
  813.6--dc23
                          2013001727

TABLE OF CONTENTS

CLAWED BY OLD GRAY

"Old Gray's back," Tray said, peering out at the scraggly gray cat squatting in his backyard.

His mom set down her knitting and hurried over to the window. "That's it, I'm calling Animal Control."

Tray glared at the cat. The cat glared back, its eyes a glowing amber with small black slits.

"They won't be able to catch him," he said.

"But he's ruining my flower bed."

Old Gray had a lot of nerve using their flower bed as a public toilet. He'd slung dirt all over the patio and twice he rooted up some of Tray's mom's blooming asters.

Tray sighed. "I'll chase him away . . . again."

In the past, he only had to open the door to spook the cat. Old Gray didn't seem to like humans. Any sound of Tray approaching and that cat flew into action, springing over the fence and jetting away.

But this time when Tray went out, the cat stayed right in the middle of his mom's prize roses. He flung dirt like a raging bull.

"Stop it!" Tray yelled, rushing over.

Old Gray halted, but he didn't scram. He stared up at Tray with hooded eyes. *You don't scare me*, he seemed to say.

Tray grabbed the long spatula by the outdoor grill and poked the handle at the cat. "Scat!"

Old Gray didn't budge.

The cat raised his hackles and hissed. His ears slicked back so far that his head resembled a snake about to strike.

"Scat!" Tray hollered again.

A menacing growl rolled out of Old Gray's throat. It was a warning that said, *Don't mess with me, boy.*

Tray didn't get it. Why was the cat being so stubborn? Was their flower bed really the best potty on the block? He looked at the spatula in his hand. *Mom will hate this, but . . .* He dug it into the ground and pitched some loose dirt at Old Gray, careful not to hit his eyes.

The grungy old cat flinched, but he didn't flee. Some of the dirt showered off his side, though most stuck to his matted fur.

Tray inched closer. He had never been this close to Old Gray before. Gross! The cat was a grungy mess. His steel gray hair was a tangle of knotted clots. There were some bald spots – probably battle scars from fighting other stray cats. His crooked tail must have been broken once or twice. But it was his teeth and claws

that made Tray freeze. Both were equally large, pointed, and ready to tear into his flesh.

This only made Tray madder. "You're not going to get away with this. I want you out of my yard now!" he hollered.

Tray rushed around and grabbed Old Gray from behind. He meant to snatch him up and toss him over the fence. It wouldn't hurt. Cats always land on their feet.

But when Tray clutched the sides of the scuzzy old thing, it flipped over in his hands. Old Gray bared his claws and sank them right into Tray's arm.

"OW!"

Tray tried to turn him loose, but Old Gray had buried his claws deep. Prying them loose was like ripping barbs from his flesh. The pain blazed though Tray's veins, causing tears to form in his eyes. He finally slung the cat away.

Old Gray crouched back, looking at Tray with victory in his glimmering eyes. Then just as quickly, he shot away, up and over the fence.

The ten holes in Tray's skin were now streaming rivulets of blood. Lots of blood! It poured out quickly, pattering onto the dirt. He rushed to the back door, holding his arm out so it didn't dribble on his clothes.

"Mom!"

Tray's mom ran out, her face turning white when she saw him. "Oh no. Stay right here. I'll get a wet rag."

The blood ran thicker, beating the ground where it fell. Tray grew weak just looking at it. His head felt like a balloon losing air. *I can't pass out.*

Mom soon returned with ice, a rag, Band-Aids, and ointment.

Tray took them from her. "I can do it." He wasn't going to let Old Gray get the best of him. He'd be tough.

After using the rag and ice to stop the bleeding, he looked at the tiny holes in his arm. They reminded him of teeny bugs burrowing into his skin. And why were there thin blue streaks snaking off from each one? He quickly applied the ointment. *Can't let this fester.*

He fumbled with the Band-Aids until Mom took over to help him out. It's hard to stick on a Band-Aid one-handed.

After the doctoring was done, Mom ran her fingers through Tray's curly black hair. "I called Animal Control. They'll be patrolling the neighborhood."

Tray looked down at his punctured arm. "I hope they brought armor."

WEIRD NIGHTMARES

That night, Tray was plagued with weird nightmares. In one, the holes in his arm had turned into blinking amber eyes and the hair on his knuckles sprouted cat whiskers.

In another dream, he was trapped in a room full of fun house mirrors. In each one he saw Old Gray's reflection, warped and twisted and ready to rip him to shreds.

Then he dreamed his arm turned a putrid yellow and swelled to the size of a tree trunk. He saw himself fading into sleep as a surgeon held up a saw, ready to hack off his bloated arm. Old Gray sat at the end of the operating table, grinning like the Cheshire Cat.

Tray woke in a pool of sweat. He quickly examined his arm. Not swollen. Not yellow. Not even sore.

He ripped off one of the Band-Aids. "Ouch!" He screamed. Some of his hair came off with it. But he let out a sigh of relief when he saw that the wound underneath was barely noticeable. The hole was just a teeny scab with no blue snakes or ooze or any of the things in his nightmares.

His mom rushed in, frantic. "What's wrong?"

He held up the Band-Aid.

"Oh." She slumped. "Please try not to scream when you take off the others."

He looked down at the remaining nine. Yikes! He nearly screamed just thinking about it! But he held his breath and yanked them off—quick, quick, quick. Though his arm stung from Band-Aid removal, he was happy to see that the rest of the holes were just as clean as the first. He hopped out of bed and went down for breakfast.

Tray sat down to his usual breakfast of Toasty Oats and orange juice. Somehow it didn't sound too tasty this morning. He poured it back into the carton and got a glass of milk instead. When he poured the milk on his Toasty Oats, he filled the bowl all the way to the rim—more milk than cereal. *That's okay*, he thought. Or was it? Why was he craving milk?

Tray ate all the cereal, then poured more milk into the bowl. He lifted it to his mouth, lapping up every drop. He licked his lips— *Yum!*—then set it down.

Mom stood by the stove, eyes wide. "Thirsty?"

It was then that he realized what he'd done. "Uh . . . yeah."

"Next time use the glass."

He smiled, sheepishly. "Okay."

After getting dressed, Tray wanted to go out and play ball with his friends. It was only June. The whole lazy summer stretched out in front of him. But he felt sluggish. *Must be from all the nightmares,* he thought. So instead of rushing out the door, he curled up on the couch for a nap.

"Aren't you feeling well?" Mom asked as she twiddled her knitting needles.

Since the yarn was pink, Tray worried that she was knitting him some more bulky itchy socks. Gah!

But he only worried for a moment. His eyes grew heavy and within seconds he was purring in Dreamland.

No nightmares now—just strange images and scenes flashing through his mind.

Tray saw himself walking along the top of a fence. Wow! He slinked across without a slip or stumble. He took his time, peering into backyards and taunting the neighbors' dogs. They yelped and barked, but Tray just grinned and carried on.

In another dream he climbed a tree—up . . . up . . . up—higher than he'd ever gone. Even the smallest branches supported him. He looked down at his friends with their balls and bats. For some reason, he preferred hanging out in the tree instead of hanging out with them.

But then came the weirdest dream. Tray was sitting, watching TV, when suddenly a rope dropped down from the ceiling. He couldn't see exactly where it came from or why it was even there. It just . . . dangled. He grabbed the rope and yanked. More rope dropped down. He tugged again, revealing even more rope. He continued pulling. *Is there no end to this?*

Eventually, the rope became a jumbled heap around his feet. It wound around him, tangling and knotting. But that didn't stop him from pulling.

"Tray!" He snapped out of his dream and sat up. His mom gazed at him, her eyes wide. She let out a long sigh. "What have you done?"

Tray blinked a few times then looked down. *What have I done?* he wondered. While sleeping, he'd somehow clutched onto his mom's yarn. It was everywhere! Not only had he unwound most of it from the ball, he'd undone all her knitting, too.

"How is this possible?" she asked. "I was only gone for five minutes."

"Uh . . . uh . . . " Tray had no idea. "I did it in my sleep."

She came over and tried uncoiling it from around him. "I think it's time for you to get up. You won't get a wink of sleep tonight."

Somehow, Tray knew that was true.

TRAY TRANSFORMS

That night Tray stared up at the ceiling. He couldn't sleep. But not only was he awake, he was alert! His light was turned off, yet everything in his room was highly visible. Including his superhero action figures that sat on the shelf in the darkest corner.

This is weird.

Even weirder, every sound in the house was twice as loud. The ticking of the clock. The rumble of the water heater. The hum of the refrigerator. Had he even noticed these noises before? Each one made his ears twitchy.

And his nose . . . Why was he still smelling the baby peas from dinner? Peas? Really? Who smells peas?

What is going on?

Right then, his arm began to itch fiercely. When he reached over to scratch it, his fingers raked over something more than claw marks. He bounced out of bed and flipped on the light. What he saw made him woozy and weak. Each tiny hole now sported silky black hair. Not like the usual hair on his arm. No, this looked a lot like fur.

Tray gulped back his fear. *Get a grip. It's not what it looks like.*

He tiptoed to the bathroom and dug a pair of tweezers from the drawer. Probably just lint. That's why it's itching.

But when he plucked one, it stung so badly his eyes watered. He gritted his teeth and tweezed another. And another. And another. Until he realized—*Holy hair balls!*—for every one he plucked several more grew in its place.

Fur was growing before his very eyes. He blinked rapidly. *I must be asleep. That's it. I'm dreaming.*

To test it, Tray grabbed about a dozen of the black hairs with the tweezers. One . . . two . . . three . . . He yanked. Ahhhhh! If he hadn't been awake, he was now. And the fur was rapidly taking root.

He leaned against the sink, gasping for breath. His head felt light. *This can't be happening!* He steadied himself, taking deep breaths. The last thing he needed was to pass out and knock his head on the toilet.

What am I going to do?

Then he caught a glimpse of himself in the mirror. What? A set of white whiskers had blossomed from his lip.

He staggered back, his heart racing. He didn't have to ask himself what was happening.

He knew. Old Gray had cursed him and now Tray was turning into a cat.

He leaned in, studying his features. *This is crazy!*

His eyes shifted and narrowed—going from oval to oblong. Their color faded from chestnut brown to laser yellow.

Tray's nose retracted into a curvy pink *T* as his lips ballooned like a chipmunk's.

He only had a moment to panic when soft black fur sprouted from every pore!

And just as quickly, Tray began to shrink lower and lower and lower. He tried to scream, but it came out, "Reaow!"

He froze. *I can't risk waking Mom. What would happen if she saw me like this?*

He leaped up onto the basin and looked at himself in the mirror. What looked back was a sleek, black tomcat with snowy, white whiskers.

If he hadn't been so freaked out, he would've thought it was cool. He arched his back and hissed. Yeah. Freaky, but cool.

Tray sat back on his haunches and thought, *Now what?* He had so many questions and the only one who could answer them was his new enemy—Old Gray.

STALKING HONCHO

Tray sprang down from the basin. He padded through the hall and into the kitchen. Above the sink was a small window that opened out. He swatted at the latch until it popped free. Pushing through the window was easy. He dropped down, landing softly on his four paws.

This is so strange!

He bounded across the yard, jumped the fence, and found himself standing next to the street. *Is this really my street? It's gigantic! The world is a different place when you're only a foot tall.*

Now wasn't the time for pussyfooting. Tray scurried down the sidewalk, checking between houses and up in trees. He double-checked the garbage cans. Old Gray had to be around here somewhere. If it took all night, he'd find him.

Wait. I'm searching in the wrong places. Old Gray's an alley cat.

And where would he find an alley cat? Easy.

Tray left his neighborhood and headed to First Street, or as his mom called it, "Fast Food Row." It was the place to go for burgers, pizza, tacos, or fried chicken. And behind every single restaurant was a humongous, stinky dumpster. Old Gray probably scrounged around back there at night, looking for tossed out taquitos and spicy sausage balls. But it was too risky to hang out there during the day. That's probably why he hid out in Tray's neighborhood, using his mom's flower bed as a toilet.

Even if I'm a cat forever, Tray told himself, *I will not potty on the petunias.*

Tray raced down the street, loping along on his slender paws. He'd never felt so light. It was like running on air. Like sailing on a breeze. Like—

Hoooooooonk!

Tray didn't know which was louder, the squeal of the car's horn or the screeching of its brakes. With his new cat reflexes, he shot back onto the sidewalk. *Phew!* His first night as a cat and he was close to being roadkill. He had a sudden vision of himself flattened, tire tracks etched along his spine. He shivered at the thought. Time to perk up and pay attention.

He made it safely to Fast Food Row. He had to be careful. A couple of the restaurants were still open. He couldn't risk any of the owners seeing him. But before he could slink back to the alley, the door to Pizza Paradise opened and out strolled Alison Davis . . . the hottest girl in school! Her hair was the color of honey

(Not the dark hazelnut kind. The golden kind in the teddy bear bottle). Her soft eyes were a denim blue. And her lips reminded him of a Valentine heart.

Tray couldn't resist. Turning on his best tomcat attitude, he pranced right up to Alison, arched his back, and rubbed his sleek body against her legs. This was the closest he'd ever get. She was definitely out of his league.

"Get away!" she hollered. Then stepping back on her right foot—*Umph!*—she punted him about four feet in the air.

Ow! The blow to his side knocked the wind right out of him. But the upside of being a cat was he landed on his feet.

Alison hurried over to her parents and stormed away.

I'm glad I'm a black cat. I hope it brings her bad luck, Tray thought.

Tray shook off the pain in his ribs and walked around to the alley. The dumpsters were lined up like train cars.

Old Gray has to be here somewhere.

He padded carefully, looking left and right. As he crossed some crates, he heard, "Watch your step."

He jerked around. "Who said that?"

Two glassy green eyes peered out from deep in the shadows.

"Who's there?" Tray called.

"Me." Out crept a scrawny tabby cat with dingy fur the color of oatmeal. He was mostly skin and bones.

Tray relaxed. This poor cat didn't seem like the bullying type.

"What's your name?" the cat asked. "Wait, don't tell me. Let me guess." He came close to Tray's face. Nearly nose to nose. "Is it Whiskers?"

Tray crossed his eyes, looking down at his bristly white whiskers. They practically glowed in the dark. "No, my name is Tray."

The cat sat back on his haunches and narrowed his eyes. "Tray? What kind of name is that?"

"It's better than Whiskers. What's yours?"

"They call me Mouser. I'm a pro at catching mice. Hungry?"

Tray gagged. "Not really. And I prefer fish sticks anyway."

"I just wondered," Mouser said, "because . . ." Before Tray knew what was happening, Mouser shot around behind him and latched onto a squirming gray mouse. "Hmmm."

All Tray could see was a tail poking out of the cat's mouth. "You're not going to swallow it whole, are you?"

Pah! Mouser spit it out. The scared little rodent ran for his life. Mouser waggled one of his scraggly eyebrows. "Nah. I just ate."

Tray was afraid to ask him what.

"What brings you back here?" Mouser asked.

"I'm looking for Old Gray."

Mouser licked a paw. "Never heard of him."

"That's the name I call him," Tray said. "He's a large, nasty beast with razor-like claws."

Mouser perked up. "Oh, that's Honcho. No one goes near him. He's mean."

"I know. But I have a score to settle with him."

"You better leave it alone, Tray. Honcho shows no mercy," Mouser warned.

Tray thought about the bloody holes in his arms. "Neither will I. Want to come with me?"

"Sure. But the first sign of him and you're on your own."

Tray nodded. "Fair enough."

Tray and Mouser spent the next few hours cruising the neighborhoods. Mouser caught three more mice, just for sport. Tray got a wad of gum and a peppermint stuck to his tail. And they both were shooed away by a trucker who was unloading crates of cabbages behind the supermarket. But no Honcho.

It was nearly dawn when Tray started to tremble.

"What's happening to you?" Mouser asked, backing away.

Tray wasn't sure, but it felt like he was growing taller. "Uh . . . I've got to go!"

"Wait!" Mouser called. "Are we going to hang out again tonight?"

Tray didn't answer. He was flying as fast as his feet could carry him.

The growing pains grew stronger. At times he thought he might burst right out of his black, furry skin. No! He wanted to change back into Tray, but not miles from home.

He heard crackling noises inside him. Things were shifting. He was aware that his whiskers had disappeared and his tail was shrinking inch by inch.

Luckily, Tray made it back to his house before the worst could happen. He pushed open the kitchen window. But just before entering, he had the feeling someone was behind him. He jerked around. Old Gray was perched on the fence, smirking at him.

"When I'm done with you, they'll call you Hopeless instead of Honcho," Tray threatened. He jumped inside his house and rushed to the bathroom.

Once he was tall enough to face the mirror, he sighed. It was him. The real him.

What a nightmare!

Tray crawled into bed and fell fast asleep. But a few hours later he woke up, choking and gagging.

What?

He coughed and spewed. Something was stuck in his throat. And just when he thought he couldn't draw another breath —*puh!*—he spit up a fur ball.

A NIGHT WITH MOUSER

When Tray woke up again, the noonday sun was peeking through the blinds. He rubbed his eyes and stumbled to the den.

"Finally!" his mom said. "I thought you might sleep all day."

So did he. "Why didn't you wake me up?"

Mom tilted her head and smiled. "I was going to, but you looked so peaceful all curled up on the bed."

Curled up? Gah!

"Hungry?" Mom asked.

His stomach gurgled. "Yeah."

Mom hopped up from her chair. "I'll make some sandwiches."

Tray dropped down onto the couch. The events of last night played in his head. So did lots of questions. *What happened? How was it possible? Will it happen again?* He ran his hand across his face, touching his eyelids, nose, and mouth. He checked his hands and feet. Luckily, he was still human. *That was it*, he decided. *It's over.*

Mom called from the kitchen. "Come eat."

His stomach gurgled again. "What are we having?"

"Tuna," she said.

Yum! His mouth watered. He bounced off the couch and raced to the kitchen like it was his last meal. It smelled so good! *Wait! I don't like tuna sandwiches.* But he ate two, washing them down with a huge glass of milk.

He burped and scooted back from the table. Ugh. Maybe it wasn't over!

* * *

That night, Tray sat on the floor, rolling a ball against the wall—over and over and over. It was a fun game between him and the wall. But it also helped him concentrate. The change was coming, he was sure of it. And he had to be prepared.

Time for a checklist.

1. Getting out of the house.

He propped the kitchen window open so he wouldn't waste time pawing at the latch.

Check.

2. Getting back home in time.

He didn't want to shift back into boy-mode and get caught wandering the streets in the wee hours of morning. So, he slipped his old

Batman watch from its plastic band, tied it to a short string, and set the alarm for five a.m. That should alert him in plenty of time. This time, no close calls.

Check.

3. DON'T FREAK OUT!

He couldn't check that one.

Tray went back to rolling the ball and waiting. What was only minutes felt like centuries. Then suddenly, his insides twisted and cramped. And slowly, he began to shrink.

His skin tightened and his fur grew. In keeping with his checklist, he didn't freak out. He clumsily slipped the watch around his neck and snuck to the kitchen. With one huge leap, he was over the sink and out the window.

There was no moon out and the night sky was a deep black. But with cat vision, that was no problem. He slinked across the yard, keeping an eye out for Old Gray.

Nothing.

Of course not. That would be too easy, he thought. *I'll find you, you old scoundrel.*

Tray jumped over the fence, rounded the corner, and—CRACK!—butted heads with Mouser.

Tray's cat eyes blurred. "Ow! Watch out!"

Mouser looked a little stunned, too. He made a coarse purring sound while still clutching a tiny field mouse in his teeth.

"How'd you know where I lived?" Tray asked. He didn't really care about the answer. But he knew Mouser would have to drop the little guy to reply. Why tease the poor mouse?

"I followed you back last night," Mouser answered. The mouse dropped to the ground and scurried to freedom.

Tray sat back. "Where do you live?"

Mouser looked away. Then Tray got it. Mouser didn't live anywhere. He spent his time behind restaurants and garbage bins foraging for food.

"Are you coming with me?" Tray asked, eager to change the subject.

Mouser gave him a mousy grin. "Of course. You need someone to look out for you."

Mouser narrowed his eyes and moved close. "What's that hanging from your neck?"

"An emergency alarm."

Mouser sniffed it. "What kind of emergency?"

Tray couldn't explain. No way would Mouser believe he was human. "Never mind. Let's go find Honcho."

The two strolled behind the fences.

"Why are you looking for Honcho?" Mouser asked. "It's like asking for trouble."

Tray kept his eyes forward, searching left and right. "It's personal."

"Okay, fine. Don't tell me."

Tray shook his head. "You wouldn't believe me if I did."

"Fine. But maybe you can shout it to me while Honcho is shredding you into confetti."

Tray glared at him. "I'll be doing the shredding."

The two cats traipsed through alleys and parking lots, peered under cars and bushes. Tray was thinking only of Old Gray. But Mouser didn't have much of an attention span. He just padded along, asking lots of questions like:

"Why do you think people gut fish before they eat them? Guts are the best part."

"Which is the better scratching post? A fence rail or a bike rack?"

"What's your favorite pizza topping?"

Tray wasn't in the mood for a pop quiz, but he didn't want to be rude. He liked having Mouser around. So he answered:

"People puke fish guts."

"A bike rack has no hidden nails that'll poke you."

"Sausage."

Then Mouser asked a whopper, "Who owns you?"

Tray paused. "Uh . . . nobody."

"Somebody must. You stay in that nice brick house."

"Uh . . . er . . . " Tray wasn't sure how to answer.

"And you're lucky," Mouser went on. "The lady who owns the house looks so nice. She owns you, right?"

Tray sat back on his haunches. "Mouser, that lady is my mom."

Mouser drooped. "She must take good care of you."

"Yeah," Tray said, wondering what Mom would do if she saw him now. "She's the best."

"And," Mouser said as they started walking again, "I bet you have a really nice litter box."

Tray froze. "What?"

Mouser twitched his nose. "How else could you resist pottying in that great flower bed?"

"Aaarrgh!" That reminded him of why he was here. "Let's go find Honcho."

Tray shot out across the street and—
HOOOOONK!

HONCHO DISCOVERED

"Ahhhhhh!"

Mouser grabbed Tray by the scruff of his neck and jerked him out of traffic. "You were nearly creamed by that SUV!"

Tray's heart pounded. "People drive so fast," he gasped.

"You've got to look both ways, man. People don't pay a lot of attention to the road."

So true! Tray thought. After catching his breath, he said, "Let's go." He looked left, then right, then bounded across the street.

Mouser followed. He didn't say much for a while. Then he asked, "Do you think your nice owner would let me stay there, too?"

"I don't think so, Mouser."

"But I wouldn't eat much. Or shed. Or kick up dust in the litter box."

"It's not that," Tray said.

"Then why not?"

What had Tray gotten himself into? His life was a wreck. He needed to find Old Gray. He needed things to get back to normal. What he didn't need was Mouser causing extra problems.

"You know," Tray said, "I'm the one who has a problem with Honcho. You don't have to tag along."

Mouser's whiskers drooped. "Are you trying to get rid of me?"

"No. It's just that . . . that . . . I'm afraid of what will happen when we find him. I wouldn't want you to get hurt."

"I wouldn't want you to get hurt either," Mouser said.

"But Honcho's a mean old tomcat. Being with me could trigger bad luck for you."

Mouser sat back. "Uh-huh. And being without me could trigger bad luck for you. Who else is going to pull you out of heavy traffic?"

Good point. "Okay. But let's concentrate on finding—*Bleep. Bleep. Bleep. Bleep.*

"Your alarm is going off," Mouser said.

Like Tray really needed him to point that out. He tapped the watch stem with his claw to shut it off. "Gotta go!" he yelled. And before Mouser could say another word, Tray scurried away.

He raced with a fury. A lonely train whistle sounded in the distance. Tray thought about the engineer on board. He was going about his business, making sure the cargo got from Point A to Point B.

"Humph," Tray said to himself. "His life is ordinary. He doesn't have to worry about turning into a furry feline late at night."

Tray was determined to find Old Gray and make life ordinary again. But he'd have to get through another day first. Just as he entered his room, he towered back up into his old self.

Ew! He hadn't bathed since yesterday and his armpits smelled like sweat stew. It stunk so bad his whiskers drooped! Whiskers? Before he flew into a panic, they retracted back into his face.

He went into the bathroom and stood under a hot shower. It was nice to be out of all that fur.

He slept in again. When he went into the den, Mom was knitting.

"Stupid Cat!" she yelled.

Tray nearly jumped out of his snug and cozy skin. "What?"

She stopped and looked up. "That stupid cat. You should see what he did to my azaleas."

Tray exhaled. *That stupid cat.* "Honcho was here?"

Mom's eyebrows dipped. "Honcho?"

"Oh . . . uh . . . I mean Old Gray. Is he gone?"

She nodded. "I called animal control, but it was too late. He'd gone off to destroy someone else's property, I guess."

Tray walked to the window and peered out. Whoa! It looked Old Gray had jackhammered the whole flower bed!

This was more than just an evil cat causing mischief. This was a personal message to Tray: *Just try to stop me.*

* * *

"Third time's the charm," Tray said to himself that night as he waited to change into a cat.

This was starting to feel routine—a routine he desperately wanted to break.

Soon Tray transformed—flesh to fur—and was ready to end this for good.

Mouser was waiting just on the other side of the fence. "I think I know where Honcho hangs out."

"Where?" Tray asked, hoping it wasn't a game of cat and mouse.

"The train depot."

Tray stopped. "Why didn't you tell me this before?"

Mouser arched into a shrug. "Because I didn't think of it until now. It's not like I follow him around, asking for trouble."

It made sense. There were lots of empty train cars to sleep in.

"Let's get going," Tray said.

For once it was nice, knowing where they were headed. No wandering. No guessing. *Please let Old Gray be there.* Tray had a feeling something big was about to happen. And that something would change him back into a boy, or keep him a cat forever.

His fur hackled and he shuddered. Cats are fine as pets, but he couldn't stand the thought of staying one . . . even if they do have nine lives.

They finally made it to the depot. The tracks crisscrossed and curved, and the steel rails were cool under the pads of his feet.

"This way," Mouser said, pushing forward.

They crept along, scouting, snooping, and searching. Suddenly . . . movement!

Tray shot out toward it . . .

THE ENDING IS UP2U!

If you think Tray and Mouser get captured, keep reading on page 53.

If you want Tray to face off against Honcho, go to page 63.

But, if you think a dog is waiting to attack Tray and Mouser, go to page 74.

ENDING 1: CAUGHT!

Tray only made it a few feet when something tightened around his neck, jerking him back. He felt like a trout on the end of a fishing pole. Only it wasn't a fishing pole, it was a snare pole. The kind used by the animal control department. A snaggletoothed guy with sagging pants held the other end.

Tray tried to turn back, but saggy-pants held the pole tight. Tray might as well have been a marionette on strings.

"Mouser!" Tray called.

"Over here."

Mouser was caught, too. His skinny body drooped and his eyes sunk.

The man controlling Mouser had a face full of pimples and shaggy dark hair. He grinned over at Saggy. "Are we good, or what?"

Saggy's eyes squinted as his face split into a smile. "I like bringing in cats. Especially the ones that try to fight."

Shaggy swiped his hair off his forehead with the back of his hand. "Mine doesn't look like much of a fighter."

"He doesn't look like much of nothing," Saggy snorted. "You can see his ribs."

Tray fumed. He wanted to fight back, but he wouldn't give Saggy the pleasure. And with this tight loop on his neck, it was pointless. But he didn't like what those two bullies were saying about his friend. Sure, Mouser was a street cat, but he was more than "nothing."

Saggy and Shaggy led them both to the truck.

Yikes! This would be no limousine ride. The back was closed in tight—no windows or bars, just some slotted vents. They were okay for breathing, but Tray wouldn't be able to look out. It'd be like riding in an ice cream truck without the Popsicles and fudge bars.

"Let's get these filthy strays to the pound," Shaggy said.

Saggy paused. "Wait. Mine's wearing a collar." Hand over hand, he reeled Tray toward him, then grabbed the scruff of Tray's neck with his bulky black glove. "Ha! Look at this!" He spun Tray around toward Shaggy. "He's wearing a Batman watch."

Shaggy laughed. "Guess he's out here fighting crime."

Tray wanted to hiss, claw, and tear at Saggy's sagging pants. But it was an impossible task while hanging in someone's grip.

Saggy popped open the back and tossed Tray in. Before he could make a break for it, Shaggy flung Mouser in too—right on top of him.

Tray had been through some embarrassing moments in his life, but this had to be the icing on the cake. Mouser slunk to the corner, his head down.

Then they waited.

Tray padded over to where Mouser sat. "Don't worry, I'll get us out of this."

But Mouser stayed quiet, giving Tray a hopeless look. Pretty soon the truck was moving and they were headed for the pound.

Saggy and Shaggy wasted no time getting there.

"In you go," Shaggy said as Tray and Mouser were tossed into separate pens.

"We've got to get out of here," Tray said.

Mouser's eyebrows dipped. "We can't. We're stuck. And by this time tomorrow . . ."

There was no need for Mouser to finish the sentence. Tray knew no one would rescue them. And cats that weren't rescued. . . He didn't want to think about that.

Just then the doors opened and another animal control officer came in, holding a whiny, frantic cat.

Old Gray! And he was mewing and crying like a coward.

Once he was locked in, Tray yelled, "You! You're the reason I'm in this fix."

Old Gray ignored him. He was too busy flinging himself against the cage door and squealing, "Help! Help! Somebody get me out of here! I'm too young to die!"

Tray sat back on his haunches, trying to think. Then—*bleep . . . bleep . . . bleep*—his alarm went off. Now what? The cage was about four times too small for his human body. If he changed now he'd be crushed. He slipped the Batman watch off his neck and tapped off the alarm.

Then he noticed the latch on the cage. It was just like the one on his kitchen window. He pawed at it until—*click*—it came loose.

Tray wasn't sure where exactly the animal control center was, but he was pretty sure it was far from his home. He should get moving while he had four paws to carry him. But he had Old Gray just where he wanted him. It was time to set things right.

He sprang up next to the sniveling cat's cage. "Not so tough now, are you?" Tray taunted.

The once evil villain now looked like a blubbering glob of fur. "I'm doomed! Doomed!"

"Not necessarily," Tray said. "I could let you out."

The cat's ears perked up. "You'd do that?"

"On one condition."

"Anything," Old Gray begged.

Tray stared him in the eyes. "You reverse this curse."

"Sure! No problem." Old Gray crawled forward. "Stick your paw through the bars."

"Is this a trick?" Tray asked.

"Just do it."

Tray slowly slipped his paw in. Then Old Gray leaned down, purred, and licked it, his rough tongue wetting the fur."

Tray gagged. "Ew!"

The older cat slinked back. "Done. Now let me out of here."

Tray looked at the spit on his paw. "How do I know—" But before he could finish, his guts twisted, his bones creaked, and like a jack-in-the-box sprung free, he popped up, back to the real Tray. He glared at Old Gray. "This better be final."

The cat looked out eagerly. His ears were slicked back like a true 'fraidy cat.

"And no more pottying in our flower bed." Tray opened the latch.

Old Gray shot out, darted across the floor, and out an open window.

Tray turned to Mouser. His good friend looked up at him with pleading eyes.

"Wait here," he said. "I promise I'll be back." Then flying as fast as he could, he ran all the way home.

He kept his promise. Later that day, he returned to the pound with his mom.

"Tray, why on earth would you want that sickly looking cat?"

"He's not sick. He just needs some decent food. We can fatten him up. And I'm sure he's great at catching mice."

"We don't have mice," Mom said.

Tray smiled. "And as long as Mouser's around, we never will."

Mom sighed. "Well, since you've already named him, I guess he's ours."

She signed a few papers and Mouser went from being alone to being loved.

On the way home, Tray whispered, "I'm going to buy you a nice big litter box. Just please stay out of Mom's flowers."

ENDING 2: THE BATTLE

"WATCH OUT!"

Tray ducked and rolled as a streak of gray flew over his head. He bounded back up on his feet. Before him stood Old Gray, his ears slicked down and his back arched. The vicious cat hissed like he'd touched a hot flame.

Tray mimicked him, arching and hissing. He refused to let this fleabag get the best of him.

"Why'd you do this to me?" he asked.

Old Gray swiped at him, barely missing Tray's eye.

I've got to get him talking, Tray thought. *If he draws more blood I could be stuck like this forever!*

Old Gray stayed quiet. He sidestepped graciously, circling Tray.

Tray kept his eyes trained on his enemy. "So what's wrong? Cat got your tongue?"

Old Gray pounced. Tray rolled away, then sprang back up to face his foe. He would not be bullied. "Why'd you curse me?"

The other cat's pupils widened as he glared.

Tray nodded. He's not the only one who can play this game. "Hey, Mouser."

Mouser had jumped onto a large crate, his body trembling. "Wh-wh-why are you talking to me?"

Tray laughed. "Because you're the only other cat that can talk back. Meathead here is too stupid to speak."

"Watch it," Old Gray hissed.

"Tha-that's good advice," Mouser stammered.

Tray ignored him. "So the idiot can speak. Amazing."

Old Gray crouched. "I can talk. But I don't have anything to say to you."

"You owe me," Tray argued.

"I don't owe you a thing. You got what was coming to you."

"Because I didn't want you tearing up Mom's flower bed? That's called vandalism. It's a crime," Tray said.

"So call the cops," the old cat smirked.

"I've got a better idea," Tray said, not daring to look away. "You reverse this curse and I won't call the pound."

"How cute. He wants to stay a real boy. Maybe you should wish on a star," Old Gray teased.

With that, Old Gray pounced. The two cats became a tangled rolling, hissing, and clawing ball.

"Get him, Tray!" Mouser cheered from his crate. "Tear him apart!"

But Tray didn't want to tear him apart. He just wanted the stubborn old cat to reverse this awful hex.

The two stayed clutched together, flipping and twisting and whirling.

In the distance, Tray could hear a train coming. He tuned it out. All he could think about right now was winning this fight.

Tray broke loose just enough to sling the cat against a handcart. Gray bounced back, knocking them both onto the track. Tray hit the rails with a humph!

The night had been as black as licorice, but suddenly there was light. Tray could see the blood matting on Old Gray's fur. But whose blood? They were both sliced up pretty bad.

"Fix me!" Tray yelled.

"I'll fix you all right," Old Gray threatened.

"Uh . . . Tray," Mouser called.

"Not now!" Tray yelled.

Old Gray sneered. "Had enough?"

"It'll be enough when I have two feet and ten toes."

"Tray," Mouser called again.

"Not now!"

"Yes, now!" Mouser hollered. The light grew stronger and—*Woo! Woo!*—a whistle blasted.

No! The train was pulling into the depot. Tray tried leaping off, but Old Gray held tight.

"Are you crazy?" Tray said. "We're about to be flattened!"

Something lit up inside the Old Gray's eyes. *Yikes!* He'd finally realized that if they didn't jump now, they'd soon be kitty burgers.

Tray leaped off, but Old Gray didn't. "Are you nuts? Come on."

The old cat's eyes widened and he looked back. Then Tray saw the problem. Gray's tail was caught in a splintered rail

Old Gray tugged. "Help!"

The train's headlight glazed the tracks as the engine grew closer and closer. *Woo! Woo!*

Old Gray grabbed his tail with his teeth and yanked. Nothing. "Get me off here!"

Tray jumped onto the track.

Woo! Woo!

Gray's tail was caught, but all Tray had to do was grab the rail with his claws and lift it up some.

"I'll free you if you promise to break the curse."

"Help me!" Old Gray pleaded.

"Not if you don't free me."

Old Gray nodded like a bobblehead doll.

"You promise?" Tray asked.

Woo! Woo!

"Yes!"

Tray pulled back the wooden rail and they both jumped to safety.

Woo! Woo!

A screeching of brakes and smell of exhaust flooded the area.

Phew! They'd made it.

"Okay," Tray said. "Do it."

Old Gray quivered, out of breath. "Hold out your paw."

Tray held up his right one, but Gray said, "No, the other one."

His left paw was practically shredded from the fight. Old Gray held up his own wounded paw. He mingled some of his blood with Tray's.

Mouser hopped down next to them. "Me next."

"Next for what?" But before Mouser could answer, Tray shed his fur and his body shot up like a beanstalk. Within seconds he had two feet and ten toes. And two hands, ten fingers, knuckles, knees, and all the rest of his human parts.

Old Gray started to slink away, but Mouser grabbed him.

What's going on? Tray wondered.

Mouser punctured a small hole in the pad of his paw and Old Gray knocked his against it. It looked like two cat's giving each other a high five.

Within seconds Mouser's oatmeal fur shed and he sprouted up, too.

Tray flinched. "Whoa!"

Mouser stretched and adjusted his New York Giants T-shirt. "Wow, it feels good to be back!"

Tray just stared, barely able to speak. "Y-y-you were human, too?"

Mouser smiled. "Yeah. But I've been stuck as a cat for about a year."

"And you didn't change during the day?"

"At first I did," he said, flexing his fingers. "But after a couple of weeks, I was meowing twenty-four-seven."

"But . . . but . . . why didn't you tell me?"

Mouser tilted his eyes toward Tray. "I was afraid you'd think I was crazy."

Tray blurted out a laugh.

"By the way, my real name is Mike."

Tray smiled. "My name is still Tray."

Mike nodded. "Yeah, that sounds more like a human name." He looked around. "I have to get home. My mom hasn't seen me in a year. She's allergic to cats."

"What about Honcho?" Tray asked.

They looked around. The old gray cat had vanished into the night.

Mike shrugged. "Oh well."

They turned and walked.

"What are you going to enjoy most?" Tray asked. "Sleeping in your own bed, eating something other than mice, or just hanging out with friends?"

Mike grinned. "I'm going to enjoy getting all those Christmas presents I missed."

They laughed and hurried on.

ENDING 3: CHEW TOYS

"WATCH OUT!"

Tray whipped around and found himself nose to nose with the ugliest bowlegged bulldog ever to walk the earth. His dumpling face had two baggy jowls, sagging like wet socks. His skin was the color of cracked concrete, and his two hooded eyes never blinked.

The dog snarled a low, grumbling *grrrrrr*. When his lips curled in, they revealed two spiked fangs jutting upward from his drooling gums.

The fur on Tray's back bristled. It only took two seconds for him to turn and skedaddle.

"Run, Mouser!" he yelled as he flew across the train yard.

Mouser shot out, racing next to him. "I'm scared to look back."

Tray could feel the dog's stinky breath huffing at his tail. "Trust me, he's right behind us."

They picked up speed, but they couldn't shake the hefty canine. Then, Tray spotted

an open boxcar hitched to an empty train. "This way!"

They cut to the left, heading straight for it. Just as they neared the door, Tray sprang high and landed on the boxcar's dusty floor. "Phew!"

But Mouser was no longer beside him.

"Help!"

The bulldog had Mouser by the scruff of his neck, shaking him like an old rag.

"Tray, help me!"

Tray thought hard. *What could he do?* There was no way he could get Mouser out of the dog's clutches.

"Got a problem?" came a raspy voice from within the shadows.

Tray turned. Old Gray sat in the corner licking his paws.

"I've got lots of problems," Tray said. "And you caused of all of them."

Old Gray shrugged.

Outside, Tray watched as the dog continued treating Mouser like a chew toy.

"Help me, Tray! Pleeeeease!"

"Your friend is in quite a pickle," Old Gray said.

Tray padded over. "Yeah. And I need to save him."

"I'm not stopping you."

"I can't do it while I'm a cat," Tray said. "You've got to remove this curse."

Old Gray scratched his chin and yawned.

"I have to save him!" Tray pounced on Old Gray, biting his ear.

"Okay, okay," the older cat said. "Chill out."

Mouser's pleas were growing distant. "Tray! Where are you? Help!"

Old Gray pushed Tray aside. "I'm bored with all this anyway." He brushed his claws lightly across Tray's paws. They tingled for a moment, then . . . Tray shed his fur and shot up to his normal human self.

He hopped off the boxcar and ran toward the dog. Poor Mouser was still being wrangled and whipped.

"Bad dog!" Tray shouted as he gathered up rocks and pelted the pooch's backside. "Put him down!"

The dog whimpered, spun, and dropped Mouser to the ground.

Tray stomped forward. "Scram!"

If the dog had a tail, he would've scooted off with it tucked between his legs.

Mouser crept over and rubbed against Tray's legs. Tray reached down, picked him up, and held him in his arms. "I'd never desert you, old friend."

The skinny cat snuggled and purred.

Before leaving, Tray went back to the boxcar. Old Gray was still there, his chin resting on his front paws.

Tray narrowed his eyes. "You listen to me, you pathetic fleabag. If I catch you trashing my mother's flower bed again, I'll send you straight to the pound. Got it?"

Old Gray yawned again. But Tray could tell it was pretend. His ear flickered with fright.

"Come on, Mouser," Tray said to his new pet. "Let's go home."

WRITE YOUR OWN ENDING

There were three endings to choose from in *Clawed!* Did you find the ending you wanted from the story? Did you want something different to happen?

Now it is your turn! Write an ending you would like to happen for Tray, Mouser, and Old Gray. Be creative!